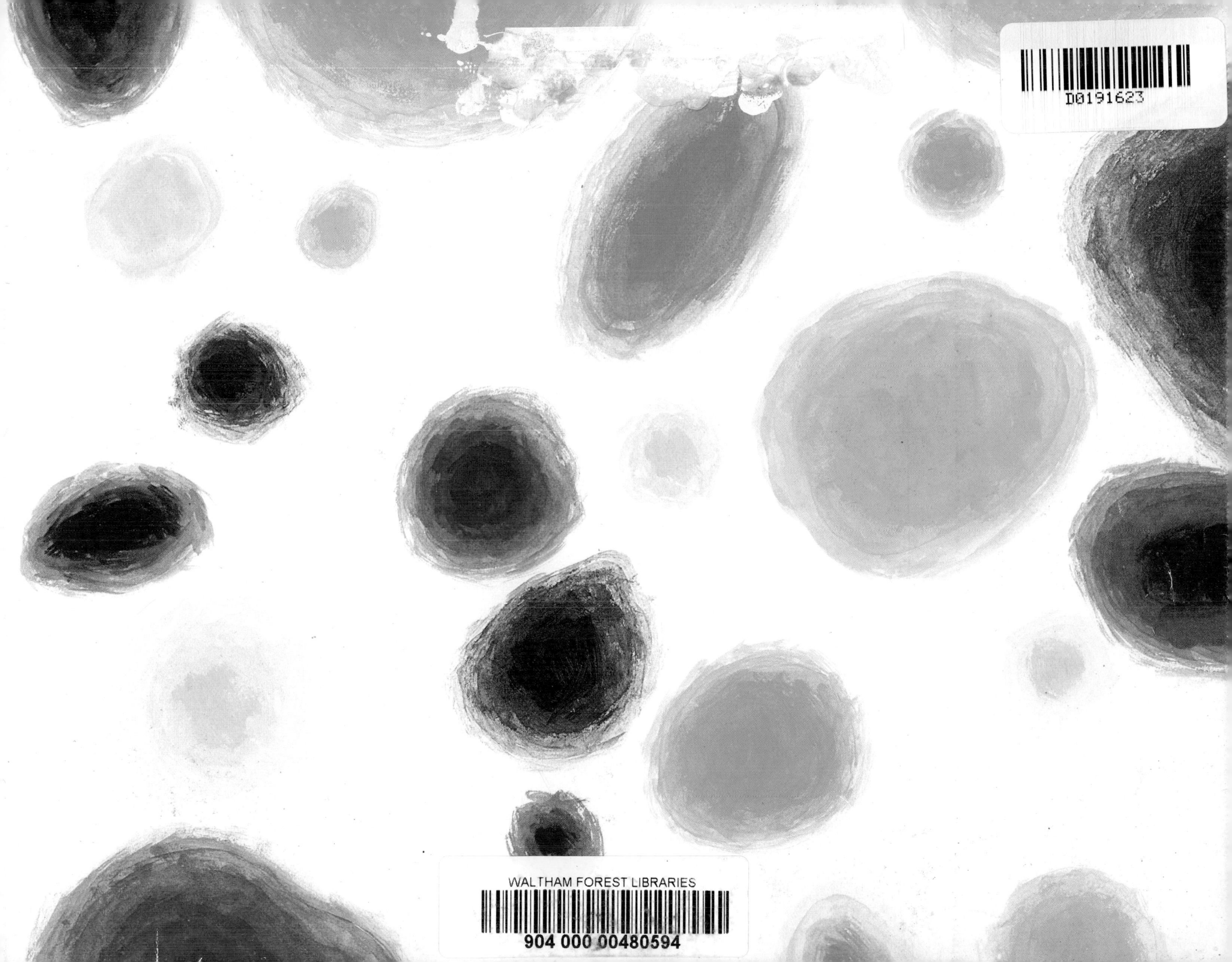

For Merm and Dayoad

First published in 2016 by Child's Play (International) Ltd
Ashworth Road, Bridgemead, Swindon SN5 7YD, UK

Published in USA by Child's Play Inc
250 Minot Avenue, Auburn, Maine 04210

Distributed in Australia by Child's Play Australia Pty Ltd
Unit 10/20 Narabang Way, Belrose, Sydney, NSW 2085

Text and illustrations copyright ©2016 Airlie Anderson
The moral right of the author/illustrator has been asserted

ISBN 978-1-84643-760-1
L100915CPL11157601

Printed in Heshan, China

1 3 5 7 9 10 8 6 4 2

A catalogue record of this book
is available from the British Library

www.childs-play.com

CAT'S COLOURS

Airlie Anderson

It was cloudy outside.
Cat was doing grey-day things.

Then she had an idea.

It was time
to collect
some colours.

She looked at the green ceiling of leaves.

She breathed
in the red smell
of the roses.

Cat reflected on the blue pond.

She noticed a flutter of purple on a branch.

As the sun set, Cat took in the orange light.

Later, she gazed at the sparkling black cosmos.

She found a cosy sleeping spot under the yellow moon.

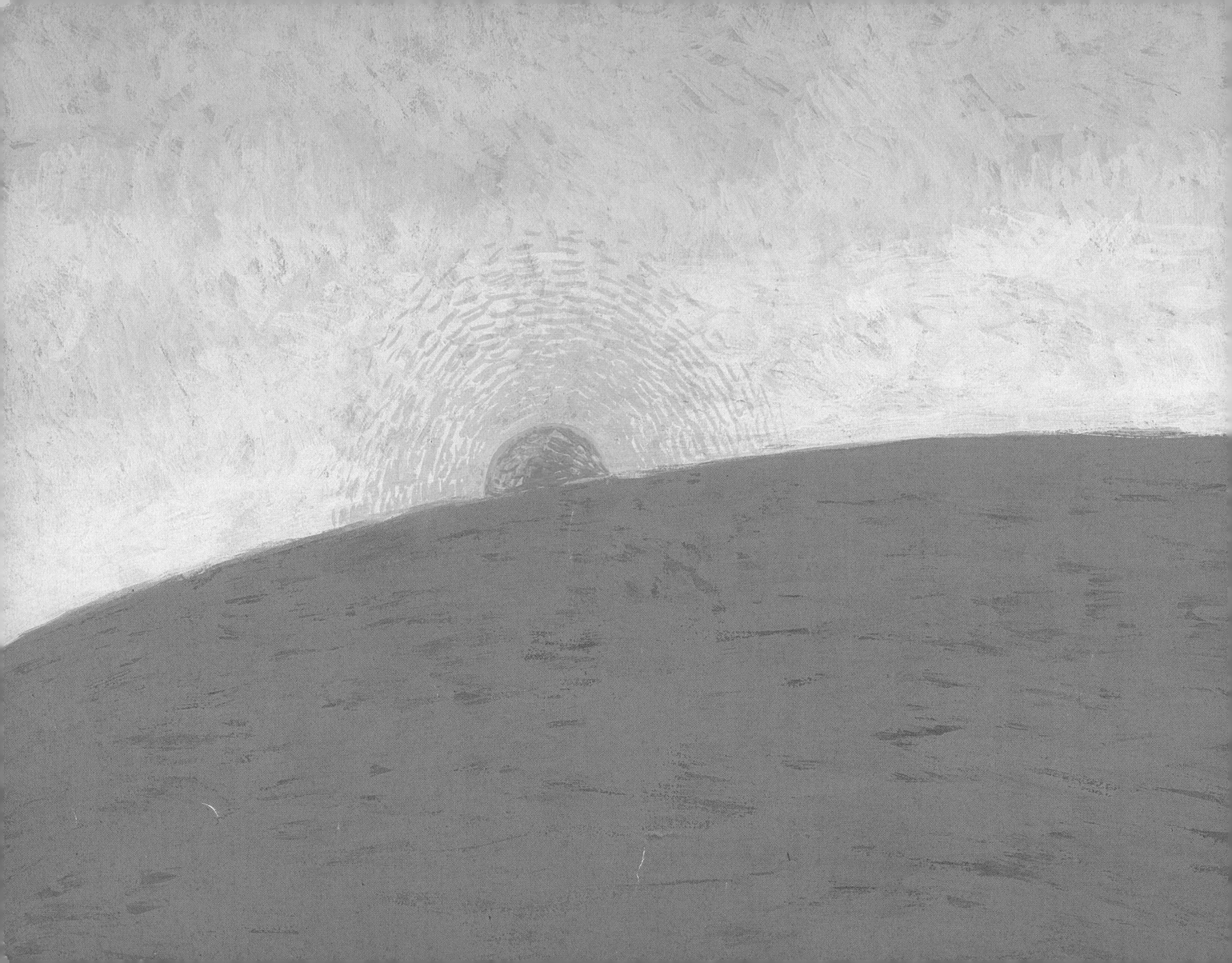

Cat?

Oh, Cat!